P9-AQX-845

JP
Willis

Remembering Barbara Niblett, who made
Burford Playgroup a happy place – J.W.

First American edition published in 2000 by Carolrhoda Books, Inc.

Text copyright © 2000 by Jeanne Willis. Illustrations copyright © 2000 by Mark Birchall.

Originally published in 2000 by Andersen Press, Ltd., London, England.

Carolrhoda Books, Inc., a division of Lerner Publishing Group
241 First Avenue North, Minneapolis, MN 55401 U.S.A.

Website address: www.lernerbooks.com

Library of Congress Cataloging-in-Publication Data

Willis, Jeanne.
    Take turns, Penguin! / by Jeanne Willis ; illustrated by Mark Birchall. - American ed.
    p. cm.
    Summary: On Penguin's first day of play school, he won't share the slide with others until Crocodile
teaches him a lesson.
    ISBN 1-57505-493-0 (lib. bdg.: alk. paper)
[1. First day of school - Fiction. 2. Play schools - Fiction. 3. Schools - Fiction. 4. Sharing - Fiction.
5. Penguins - Fiction. 6. Animals - Fiction.] I. Birchall, Mark, 1955- ill. II. Title.
PZ7.W68313 Tak 2000
[E]-dc21   00-008390

Printed and bound in Singapore
1 2 3 4 5 6 - OS - 05 04 03 02 01 00

3065200080 9212

Take Turns, Penguin!

By Jeanne Willis
Pictures by Mark Birchall

Carolrhoda Books, Inc./Minneapolis

It was Penguin's first day at school.
  "You'll like it here," said his mother.
"They've got a slide."
  And off she went.

There was no one on the slide, so Penguin climbed up and slid all the way down.

Then he did it again.
And again.

And again. Soon, there was a line
behind Penguin.

"My turn," said Rat.

"No it isn't," said Penguin, and he pushed
in front of Rat.

"My turn," said Rabbit.

"No, it's not. It's my turn," said Penguin.

And he pushed in front again.

"Teacher! Tea...cher! Penguin won't take turns,"shouted Weasel.
The teacher was busy.
"Sort it out yourselves," she said.

WHOOOOSH went Penguin.

"It's not fair!" said Warthog. "You've had eighty-six turns!"

"I was here first," said Penguin.

And he had his eighty-seventh turn.

"It's rude to push," said Parrot.
Penguin paid no attention.

"I've had enough of this," said Prairie Dog.
"I haven't," said Penguin.

And would you believe he did it again?
"What are we going to do?" sighed Elephant.
"I know…" said Crocodile.

And he lay at the bottom of the slide
with his mouth wide open.

The teacher finished what she was doing.
"Where's Penguin?" she asked.
"Teacher! Tea...cher. I know where he is.
He's inside Crocodile," said Weasel.

"Take that Penguin out of your mouth at once!" said the teacher. "Now, whose turn is it on the slide?"

"Crocodile's," said Penguin.

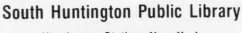